single

by philip palios

artist's statement

Hello. I like to write novels, but the past year has stretched me into territory I never intended to explore. First with poetry, then with memoir and short stories. These exercises have graced me with a new appreciation for words and language that are exemplified in the works that follow.

Through my craft I find the power to express thoughts, feelings and ideas that are impossible for me to share in any other way. My writing does not aim to entertain the reader. I seek to create works that make the world a little less occupied with the mind and a little more in love with the heart.

In the case of this chapbook, my focus lies on the complexity of relationships. I am fascinated by the myriad ways in which people come together and drift apart. I hope that these stories take the romance out of relationships and expose the guts of the beast.

For Mary

single

we look at each other
searching eyes
searching bodies
seeking a missing piece
not settling, but lonely

a stolen glance
along the pavements
where fortune lies
an offline menagerie
finding solace in coffee

venture out tomorrow
it will not be yesterday
a life exploring is not wasted
we do not know
what we're looking for

stolen pages of an autobiography

i. detroit

The heavens were full of little shrunken deaf ears. Moths were skittering out of drowning noses enveloped in flame. Infinitesimally small fireflies dripped from my right nostril, illuminating tattered ribbons that had replaced my tongue. Words were hard. I knew how to speak and I knew the words, but I didn't know where to put them so that mouth speak. Neon dancing goats, were they goats? A ray gun flew through my eye socket. Twenty-two was the most beautiful color, I wanted to smell more of it. "Where?" A word came. A word from my word mouth! And then the Gods possessed my body, rotating it through space and time so that having achieved cosmic alignment, I could see. There they were! I was the first to see them. Those little dancing beasts speaking with their fingers and waving their upside down bubble-gum. Nothingness. That's where

Altoids come from, but how do I tell Shauna? Dance,

dance, dance, dance, dance – Where does heaven come

from? If you're in space, is hell under the bedsheets? Rain

shot up my skirt and electrified my Jimi Thing. Eat. Eat.

If only I had a color under my lips, I could consume a

dozen Sonic booms. Eat sleep read dance where is

Shuana? Shut up, it's a ballad. I go up, but there is nothing

to shut, so I go down and I'm sitting in a baseball frame.

Exit stage yellow and dump that cheating motherfucker I

told her, victory was mine, but where was she? "Shauna!"

My mouth was floating underneath a raisin. The force of

God resumed changing my astral projection and I

discovered that I had been left-handed All Along the

Watchtower. She holds me down and massages my kidney

before I float away. Eat. I have no stomach, I protest without words. She coos. Found Shauna. It's Halloween.

ii. radio

"Don't touch that dial, or else I'll lose my job and so will you!"

I followed his instructions, but found them strange because I didn't have a job. Next, I was told to buy Pop Rocks and get an oil change, but I didn't have any money or a car. When DJ DJ returned, he told me he was about to drop something, so I told him that I hoped it wasn't his iPhone. He laughed.

"You're so dense Phil, or just awful at humor."

"Both actually." I responded.

The door clicked. Shauna arrived to pick me up from the studio. I did not wave goodbye.

In the car, she told me she had found me a job. I salivated. I was still thinking about Pop Rocks.

"What? What is it?" I asked.

"Starbucks is paying people to go through their drive-thrus and be rude to baristas, then report back how they respond."

Wow, I thought, noticing my jaw go slack. "Too bad I don't have a car."

"I solved that too. If you sign-up to drive with Uber, they will give you a 29 percent car loan."

"Like 29 percent off a car?"

"No, that's the interest. But they take it out of your paycheck, so it's cool. Like a company car."

"I thought company cars were free..."

"Can you stop complaining and just be glad I found you a job?"

"Yeah, um, thanks. How was work?"

"I quit."

"What?!"

"I figured it's my turn to be DJ DJ's Taco Bell bitch, now that you won't have time to hang out there anymore."

"But. Ugh, never mind." The car rolled to a halt at a four-way stop and I spotted a Quik-E Mart. "Can we buy some Pop Rocks?"

"No, we're going to another show tonight. No drugs this time, k? You completely ruined it for me last night."

"Yeah, that was awful. Thanks for having my back."

iii. friends

Where do the buffalo roam these days? And has anyone in here ever ridden on a tractor? My mind wandered. No, we come here to wear flannel and listen to folk singers tell us what it's like.

"I'm bored, I'm bored, I'm bored," I announced, but Shauna ignored me. I wished there were drugs that got me high but didn't make me intent on ruining my girlfriend's night. I looked at the stage and imagined myself leaping up there and pretending to ride a bull. "Why do we go to shows that suck, Shauna?"

"Because we can get into them for free. And these are our friends! We have to support our friends."

"So if I started singing, do you think Billy here would come to my shows?" I asked as I pointed up to the stage at Shauna's best friend from high school.

"Yeah! In fact, I do."

That's how it all started. If you told me back then
that I would become a multi-platinum rock star, I wouldn't
have believed you.

iv. hooters

My first performance was in a Hooters bathroom.
Billy didn't show. In fact, it was just me. But with such a
small bathroom, it was the perfect size crowd for me. I
sang my heart out, proclaiming my love for Shauna and
Coke bottles doused with Pop Rocks. It was a good twenty
minutes before the manager arrived and escorted me back
to the bar.

"I heard you in there," the man next to me turned in
my direction with a grin on his face that was difficult to
parse.

I stared blankly, waiting for my first review as a
professional artist.

8

"Davey. Davey Crockett. My parents were strange, but it's Davey with an 'e.'"

I shook the hand that Davey offered up, not believing for a second that it was his real name.

"Not bad. Not bad. I do promo and management for a few local musicians. Why don't you let me introduce you to a voice instructor? Maybe I can get you a real show. Give me your phone number."

Davey slid me his business card and I stared at it, nodding. I was in shock, if he was playing me it was quite an elaborate joke. I scratched my name and phone number on a napkin and handed it to him.

Returning home, I told Shauna the story and she laughed – not questioning for a second whether Davey was serious. I went to bed holding on to the possibility that he was, but with a loose grip.

The next morning, I was still wearing my pajamas when my phone rang. I didn't recognize the number and was beside myself when Davey introduced himself on the other end of the line.

"Hey kid, there's no time to waste – say I pick you up and introduce you to Gloria? She taught Bono's half-nephew twice removed."

"Yeah, yeah I'm not doing anything today anyway." I gave him my address and scrounged up some clothes from my bedroom floor.

"Who was that?" Shauna inquired.

"Davey. From last night. He's on his way to pick me up and take me to a voice lesson."

Shauna stared at me blankly. I suppose she had good reason to be in disbelief, she had yet to hear me sing.

I kissed her goodbye when Davey arrived, she remained speechless.

After a few weeks taking lessons from Gloria in-between my Starbucks escapades, I worked up the courage to have my second public performance. It was in a QFC parking lot and there were at least fifty people in attendance, most of them unwillingly. But Billy and Shauna were there and when they ran up to me after the show, both beaming with excitement, I knew that Davey was on to something.

discovering a possibility

i. showbox

I could smell the alcohol and tobacco permeating through the club. Too young to drink and too wise to smoke, these substances were nothing but obnoxious to me. I got all of their harm and none of their charm. The stage in front of me was being vacuumed as "You put the lime in the coconut" played over the loudspeakers. It was dark and the figures standing in wait for the show were faceless. There was a four-foot high metal barricade creating a narrow gap where I stood between the stage and the crowd silently holding my Nikon N80 mounted with a 50mm prime lens. Mary was somewhere back in the crowd, I searched through the unknown faces until I spotted her smile. I didn't know how I had been so lucky to be with her.

As the crowd grew denser, waves of anticipation reverberated through the tiny black-walled box of a venue. The band walked on stage to a deafening uproar of screams and shouts from everyone standing behind me. I felt like an intruder, unworthy of being in the audience, let alone standing in front of them. It took the one droplet of courage I had not to walk away. That droplet came from Mary. I had no idea why she cared for me, she was the woman of my dreams who I had thought would always be out of reach. If I felt unworthy of the place where I stood, my unworthiness of Mary was a hundredfold. House lights flashed off and stage lights faded on. Blue, green, red and white – every band received the same generic illumination. The first song started and I set to work. The singer was beautiful, singing her heart out with every note. I envied her fearlessness. As I snapped my photographs I imagined the scenes I was capturing for me and Mary to look through after the film was developed. I quickly made my way back and forth in front of the stage, gently stepping over throngs of cables running beneath me while speakers blasted mere inches from my ears. I was in my element and no longer paid any mind to the people behind me. My three-song allotment soon drew to a close and I exited the narrow channel to join Mary among the crowd. A broad grin rose across her face as I approached, her eyes, glowing, met mine. I didn't understand what it was she thought was so great about me.

Days later, I picked up the prints from the lab. It was one blurry grey or red under-exposed photograph after another. I was overwhelmed with shame. I knew I could do better than this, but the evidence suggested otherwise. If I told Mary, I knew that would be the end of things. But when I finally worked up the courage to tell her, via text message, I was shocked by her indifference. "oh well – next time will be better," her message read. If it wasn't my photography that led her to liking me, what could it possibly be?

ii. bedroom

The power shut off with a loud bang. Mary had been in the bathroom doing something to her hair and I smelled smoke. When she entered the bedroom where I had been waiting for her, I was relieved to see that her hair wasn't on fire. "What happened?" I asked, as if it wasn't obvious.

"Fuck!" she responded, clutching a hair straightener in her hand. Neither of us knew where the circuit breaker was. We were staying at her brother's apartment while he was off studying rocks in the desert for a week or two.

Looking at each other, we each expected the other person to fix the problem. Finally, her brother's roommate emerged from his room, clearly upset about his uninvited houseguests and their antics. He wandered off somewhere and then the lights came back on. We returned his death stare with a friendly "Thanks!"

Mary stayed in the bedroom with me and shut the door behind her instead of returning to the bathroom. It was mid-afternoon and the small bedroom's white walls were illuminated by a flood of sunlight coming through the window. I sat on a chair in front of her brother's desk and she sat on the bed behind me. "Don't turn around." she ordered. Her black t-shirt flew by, narrowly missing my head as I stared at her laptop sitting open on the desk. I imagined what she was doing behind me and heard her shake her jeans loose from her legs, then I heard the sound

16

of elastic and cotton sliding down her thighs. "This is going to be great. Do you know what he will think when we walk out and I'm wearing different clothes?" she asked.

Yes, of course I knew what he would think. Or at least I knew what she thought he would think. And I liked it. But I didn't really care what he thought, I just wanted what she wanted him to think to be true. Yet I kept staring at the laptop screen, scared she would run out of the apartment and never speak to me again if I turned around.

iii. car

The party was uneventful. I recall sitting on a couch and drinking a Mike's Hard Lemonade, it was all the rage while underage. We departed after a socially-acceptable amount of time had passed. I was driving my jet black 1994 Honda Accord coupe and Mary was sitting in the passenger seat next to me. She was arranging the perfect playlist on the iPod plugged into my stereo while I stared out into the vast darkness of the road ahead. Once she was satisfied, she placed the iPod in a cup holder, turned up the volume and slid back into her seat. The world passed by and I kept my hands at ten and two.

"Kiss me!" she screamed. The thoughts in my wandering mind shattered into oblivion as she repeated herself, turning her head and looking at me with a commanding gaze. I had wanted to kiss her since the moment I met her, but I never had the guts. I looked over and saw her pale white skin gleam under a passing streetlight, her red lipstick ignited my passions. I held back only because I was concerned about causing a car crash. Pulling over to the side of the road had not occurred to me.

After I turned into her neighborhood she shouted a third time, "Why won't you kiss me?" So I did. It was

18

glorious, fireworks flew high and I nearly ran into a trash

can. She reached for my hand and thrust it between her

legs.

breaking up

I chipped my tooth sometime between going out last night and eating breakfast this morning. This has happened before. It might have even been the same tooth. At first, I thought part of my breakfast had lodged itself between my teeth, but I used my tongue to pry and pick at it until I felt the nails-on-a-chalkboard texture of freshly-exposed inner-tooth. I sighed and wondered if I swallowed the missing piece or if it exited my mouth in some other fashion.

If I wasn't so good at taking advantage of nepotism, by "working" for my father in his law firm, I might have been an interior designer. There was something about making things neat, clean, organized and elegant that I had a knack for. So when Natalie told me she wanted to be an interior designer on our first date, I knew we would probably be a good match. Now, I think she might have been feeding me a line of bullshit. We've been dating for five weeks and as far as I can tell she has no ambitions in life. She goes out and parties every night. Lately, I have gone along with her more times than not. Last night, we went to a show and by the time I got home it was five in the morning. I was so drunk leaving the club that I could barely walk and had forgotten my own address. With a dead cell phone, I walked along an empty street hoping a taxi might drive by and pick me up. I was deathly tired, drenched in cigarette smoke and my ears were ringing. I lost track of Natalie and now I wanted nothing more than to lay down in my own bed.

I arrived home rather mysteriously. My flat represented everything that I was not at the time; it was spotless, smelled of lemon zest and was silent as death. A wave of solace washed over me as I entered, granting me the peace I so desperately sought. My feet wobbled and my head spun as I made my way to bed. It wasn't until I woke up this morning that I puked my guts out, with most of my vomit thankfully landing in the toilet. After downing a pot of coffee, I felt half-human and began the process of rejuvenating myself.

First, a shower. I stood under the downpour until my fingers wrinkled into raisins, basking in the warmth of the endless flow of water. Washing the sweat and grit from my pores was nothing short of a spiritual experience, but no matter how hard I scrubbed, I could not wash the ick from my soul. A soft, luscious pastel orange towel gently dried my skin before I slipped into a set of pajamas that lay neatly folded in my dresser. Looking at the pile of clothes I had shed before entering the shower, I felt like tossing them into the garbage, or at least washing them three or four times. Thankfully, they appeared to have lost the silt of a night wasted after a single run through the washer and dryer.

Natalie arrived early, ringing my doorbell at 4:23 in the afternoon for a dinner we had planned to commence at 6. I had not even left the house for the market, but I had changed out of my pajamas. Throughout the day, I ran my tongue along the chalky surface of my chipped tooth, hoping the missing piece had been magically restored.

"Fun time last night, yeah?" she asked in greeting.

"Something like that. I woke up with a pocket full of buttons and a pounding headache."

"Hah. You are such a sucker. Nice place you got here though. Neat and clean, neat and clean. You hire a maid service?"

"No, I just like to keep it clean. It's my sanctuary."

"Looks more like your hotel room to me."

I looked around at my furnishings and shrugged, "I haven't gone to the market yet. You're early."

"I wanted to see you got home safe. You ran out of the club without me. Kinda fucked up, ya know? Anyway, you can run to the market. I'll stay here and find your secrets."

I looked at the grin on her face and felt moldy. I still didn't know if I liked her and I wasn't sure if she liked me. Maybe we were just using each other for sex and entertainment. We had met on OkDateMe and the whole relationship felt a bit forced.

"Stay here? Why not come along?" I asked with a half-frown, not trusting her enough to leave her alone in my home. After a moment of silence, I nodded, "Okay sure. Back in a bit."

I ran, literally ran, to the market down the street, unsure what Natalie might do in my absence. My plan was to make a pasta with chicken, nothing complicated. Maybe a side salad. I thought that might make me appear health-conscious, which I was not.

When I returned, Natalie was naked. She sat on the couch and looked at me with raised eyebrows, legs spread wide apart. "Wanna fuck?" She asked nonchalantly.

I hesitated. It had been three days since we last had sex and I was jonesing for her, but she was sitting on my first grown-up couch. I had been so proud of myself when I bought it. No more Ikea, finally something nice to put in my living room. When they delivered it and I saw it for the first time, sitting where it still sits today, I was so enamored with its beauty I didn't even want to sit on it.

"Well, yeah – but how about we take this to my bedroom?"

"Oh, c'mon – I know you fantasize about this. Let's do it!"

"Actually, I don't fantasize about sex on my couch. I don't want to mess it up. And couch sex is awkward anyway. I'll carry you to bed."

I set the groceries by the door and approached to scoop her up in what I perceived to be a romantic gesture.

"No!" she shouted, "What's wrong with you?" kicking me away with a raised leg. I saw how smooth her skin was and nearly lost my balance. As I returned to my groceries, she stood and began picking her clothes up from the floor.

"I just don't want to get my couch dirty. You know?" I went into the kitchen and started prepping dinner.

"What's wrong with you? It's going to get messed up eventually. Let's break it in! That's what makes it yours. Your place is so static, it looks like a showroom. There is no character. I thought you wanted to be an interior designer?"

"I like my couch the way it is. Just as nice as when I bought it. That's the point, you know. Taking care of it."

"Like a museum piece. Right."

I started prepping the salad as I noticed she was now fully-dressed and putting her coat on. "Are you leaving?" I asked, frustrated that she was making such a big deal out of this.

"This isn't going to work. I thought you were different. You know, someone who liked to have fun."

I hated it when she said things like that, she was just like my ex – flipping the argument around so I was always the loser, the one at fault, the guilty party. I was pissed and didn't have the words to respond, so I grabbed the simmering sauce pan from the stove and threw it on my linoleum kitchen floor. It didn't break. There was a loud thud followed by a zinc echo and red sauce sprayed everywhere. My pants were stained with dark red sauce oozing down onto my shoes.

"Is this the character you're looking for? Are these cabinets better now? How lovely, right?" I gestured toward the oak cabinets that were now splattered with sauce. Blood rushed through my ears, I had never been this angry before. "I do like to have fun. I'm just not all for going out until five in the morning every night and coming home drenched in sweat and cigarette smoke. Waking up in the morning and having to puke, followed by discovering a piece of my tooth is missing is not for me. Or fucking on the couch. That's not fun. Going to a concert, dancing and getting home at a decent hour. Fucking in the comfort of a bed. That sounds more fun to me."

Natalie stared at me with burning eyes that made it hard to believe she was even capable of love. I wanted her to be different and was finally starting to see that she wasn't playing the part I had written for her. Our selfish gazes locked in a mutual hatred before she turned and walked out the door, slamming it shut behind her.

on efficiency

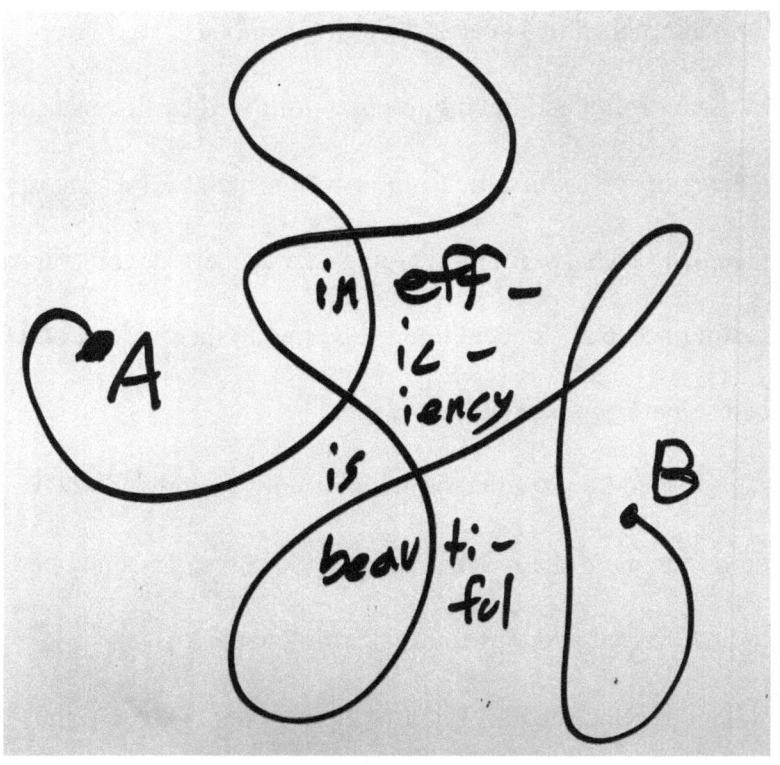

you can't just drop buildings on people

Georgia rolled over and felt her body push up
against something hard. She opened her eyes and blinked
through the morning blur, revealing the concrete base of a
massive skyscraper. Sitting up, she slapped her face, then
blinked and saw the same structure that could not possibly
be there. Thinking through the night before, she recalled
laying alongside Ella and staring up at the stars after
polishing off a bottle of cheap champagne. There had been
the same vast expanse of grass that had always been in the
park since they began their weekly ritual. The only
skyscrapers were set far in the distance. Standing up, she
looked around for Ella, but found the park unusually
vacant. Growing concerned, she began walking along the
perimeter of the building shouting for her partner.

Rounding a corner, Georgia's pace quickened as her mind raced with paranoid thoughts about entering an alternate reality, some sci-fi shit, or something else that would end with her locked up in a mental ward. Making her way around the third corner, she spotted Ella's bright pink Nikes lying beside the base of the building. Georgia ran up to the shoes and knelt down to pick them up, only to leap backwards in horror when she spotted Ella's ankles coming out of the shoes, half-buried beneath the building.

"Ella?!" she screamed frantically. Leaning back down, she grabbed the shoes and pulled, imagining that she could somehow extract her lover from the building as if it were nothing but a bouncy house. The body didn't give an inch and Georgia fell backwards in bewilderment. Recovering and rising to her feet, she began running around the building in search of an entrance. "Help! Help!

Please!" she screamed as she rounded the next corner. No one was nearby to hear her call and the building didn't seem to have an entrance. When she made it all the way back to Ella's feet, she turned and gasped in a panic "No! No! It can't – She can't."

Hyperventilating, she paused at the sound of a man's gravelly voice approaching in the distance. "How on earth did it end up here?"

"I know, I mean – it's a park!" a woman's voice responded. Georgia looked up and saw two suit-clad businesspeople approaching.

"You!" she screamed, running toward the pair, "You killed Ella!"

"Ella? Ella O'Neil?" the woman questioned.

"Yes, yeah – how do you know her name?"

"That explains it," the man answered.

"Well, you see miss – This building was intended for 1 Ella O'Neil Place. The delivery drones must have mixed up the address. The program is still in beta" the suited woman added.

"WHAT?! WHAT. THE. FUCK?! Are you serious? You deliver fucking buildings? Since when is that a thing?" Georgia was nose-to-nose with the woman.

"It's new. Like she said, it's still in beta. We're so sorry for your loss" the man answered matter-of-factly.

Georgia's blood boiled. "You can't just drop buildings on people!" she exclaimed as she pounced on the woman in the suit, knocking her to the ground. First with her right fist, then with her left, she began rapidly punching the woman in the face.

"Hey now! Hey! Calm down, now listen-" the man with the gravelly voice leaned down and grabbed Georgia by the forearm, but she was stronger than he was. She turned and punched him directly in the throat, knocking the wind out of him as he fell onto his back gasping for air.

"You fuckers drive me crazy. You are worse than the mob. You come here and shit all over this city thinking you can do whatever you want because you 'innovate.' All your little child geniuses whittling away so you can save me the trouble of having to walk down the street to buy a fucking book. FUCK YOU!" The woman who had never introduced herself was now unconscious. The man with the gravelly voice was back on his feet and slow-jogging away with his phone held up to his ear. Georgia paused and took a deep breath, playing out what might happen if the police showed up. She stood and began running in the opposite direction of the man.

10 YEARS LATER

"Georgia! It's so good to finally meet you!" Robert came bustling through the coffee shop door wearing a freshly-pressed green oxford with dark khaki slacks and a polished brown belt that matched his Clarks. "I mean, to see you in person. You're even more beautiful in real life than you are on Skype."

"Hey, you too." Georgia rose from her seat to engage in an obligatory three-second embrace.

"Do you want a coffee?" Robert pointed toward the barista while Georgia returned to her seat.

Silent, she gestured at the glass of iced tea sitting in front of her and raised the left side of her lips in a half smile.

"Right. I'll be right back. I'm so happy you're moving out here from the boonies!"

"I used to live here, you know?" Georgia was already regretting her decision to come out here and she was especially perturbed by Robert's assumption that she was moving in with him. Despite nearly a year of regular e-mail and video chat conversations, seeing him in-person made her feel as if she barely knew him.

When Robert returned, clutching a cappuccino in a paper cup, he launched into an excited verbal spew. Georgia wasn't paying attention to his words, she was looking at his heavily-gelled hair and wondering if it was flammable. His hair had always been a bit frazzled when she saw him on the computer screen, and she liked the non-conformity.

"Babe. Babe, isn't it amazing how this city is exploding?" Robert waved his hand in front of Georgia's face, having noticed her mental drift.

"Huh? Exploding? Why?" Georgia had been in the city just three hours and was already perturbed by her fellow airplane and BART passengers who reminded her of the yupster culture she had so eagerly fled ten years earlier.

"It's not like Oklahoma, ya know? Nothing stays the same for long here. You probably don't even recognize it, do you?" Robert kept asking questions and Georgia wondered why he was acting like such a patronizing asshole, he wasn't like this when they talked online. Despite his techie job, she thought he wasn't like all the other guys in San Francisco. Five minutes seeing him in person and she was slowly beginning to accept how painfully wrong she had been. Georgia chewed on her lip before responding to Robert's queries, "Did you know we have sixty earthquakes per year in Oklahoma? They're fracking the fuck out of us."

"Hah, yeah…" Robert popped a cheesy grin straight out of a toothpaste commercial, clearly uninterested. "I can't wait to show you my place. It's so legit, you won't believe it."

"Well, Robert…I came here to see you, but sure - why not?" Georgia pounded her iced tea and rose to her feet.

"Oh, now? Sure. It's just around the corner in Alta Plaza Park."

"In the park?"

"Yeah, crazy right? It was the first drone-installed high-rise in the city. I guess there was some sort of mix-up and it ended up in the wrong spot, but the city let it stay."

"Oh." Georgia swallowed hard. "Of course they did." When they rounded the corner and Georgia saw the same towering monstrosity that drove her out of the city looming over her once beloved park she nearly lost it. "It's nice." Where did that come from? Her mouth was defying her.

"Wait 'til you see inside."

As they approached the concrete base of the building, Robert pushed his hand up against the solid surface and the green outline of a door appeared. He pushed inwards, revealing a classically-decorated lobby. Georgia followed him inside and watched the door close behind them.

"I have the penthouse suite. You can see the whole city, the whole bay. It's magnificent." Robert approached the elevator and punched the button. Moments later, the doors slid open to the sound of a chime. Georgia took in the checkered marble tile floor and crystal chandelier before following Robert into the lift. As the doors were closing, she saw "Ella O'Neil Memorial Building" etched in copper above the lobby entrance. She shuddered.

When they arrived in his suite, Georgia set her purse down and blinked in awe at the floor to ceiling windows that covered all of the exterior walls. She walked up to one that looked down towards the marina and spotted the Palace of Fine Arts. She recalled countless Sunday walks with Ella around that beautiful monument.

"I'm just so happy you're here, Georgia. You're going to love being back home and saying goodbye to that dead-end job in Oklahoma. You don't even have to find a job if you don't want to."

Georgia lost her balance and caught herself against the window she was observing the city from. The day she had left replayed in her mind's eye. She grew dizzy and continued leaning against the glass as tears began rolling

down her cheek.

author bio

Philip Palios was born at home in Kirkland, Washington on May 28, 1985 and has lived in the Pacific Northwest for most of his life. After working in the high-tech corporate world for about a decade, he dropped out in July 2015 to pursue writing. His first novel, *Electric Love*, was published in May 2016.